CITIES
BUENOS AIRES

ABDO
Publishing Company

Nancy Furstinger

visit us at
www.abdopub.com

Published by ABDO Publishing Company, 4940 Viking Drive, Edina, Minnesota 55435.
Copyright © 2005 by Abdo Consulting Group, Inc. International copyrights reserved in all
countries. No part of this book may be reproduced in any form without written permission from
the publisher. The Checkerboard Library™ is a trademark and logo of ABDO Publishing Company.

Printed in the United States.

Cover Photo: Corbis
Interior Photos: AP/Wide World p. 20; Corbis pp. 1, 6-7, 8, 9, 12, 14, 15, 17, 18, 19, 22, 22-23, 24,
    25, 28, 29; Fotosearch p. 5; Getty Images pp. 11, 13, 27

Series Coordinator: Jennifer R. Krueger
Editors: Megan M. Gunderson, Jennifer R. Krueger
Art Direction & Maps: Neil Klinepier

Library of Congress Cataloging-in-Publication Data

Furstinger, Nancy.
    Buenos Aires / Nancy Furstinger.
        p. cm. -- (Cities)
    Includes index.
    ISBN 1-59197-855-6
    1. Buenos Aires (Argentina)--Juvenile literature. I. Title.

F3001.F885 2005
982'.11--dc22

                                                    2004055423

CONTENTS

Buenos Aires.. 4

Buenos Aires at a Glance................................. 6

Timeline... 7

Building a City.. 8

Powers That Be.. 14

Scary Roads! 16

Money Troubles 18

Humid City 20

Porteños 22

Free Time.. 26

What to See 28

Glossary 30

Saying It 31

Web Sites 31

Index 32

BUENOS AIRES

European elegance blends with South American spirit in Buenos Aires. Here, grand boulevards host trendy shops and tango parlors. Large colonial houses can be seen in reflections on shiny skyscrapers. To the west stretch the Pampas. These South American plains are patrolled by gauchos.

A blend of many different people makes Buenos Aires what it is today. Buenos Aires residents, or *porteños*, are a multinational group. They arrived from Europe and the Argentine countryside. They settled in barrios, or neighborhoods, that reflect their individuality.

In 1880, Buenos Aires became the capital of Argentina. Today, it is a capital city like no other. It has parks, large avenues, fashionable shops, and European **architecture**. These features earned the capital the nickname "Paris of South America."

Opposite Page: The colonial architecture of Buenos Aires reminds porteños of those who first settled there. The name Buenos Aires, which means "good winds," refers to the winds that brought the Spanish to the area.

BUENOS AIRES AT A GLANCE

Date of Founding: **1536 and 1580**

Population: **12 million**

Metro Area: **77 square miles**
(199 sq km)

Average Temperatures:
- **49° Fahrenheit (9°C)**
  in coldest month
- **74° Fahrenheit (23°C)**
  in warmest month

Annual Rainfall: **35 inches (89 cm)**

Elevation: **82 feet (25 m)**

Landmarks: **Plaza de Mayo,**
La Boca

Money: **Argentine Peso**

Language: **Spanish**

FUN FACTS

Buenos Aires's culture is a mixture of countries from all over the world. According to an old saying, people from Buenos Aires "speak Spanish, eat Italian, dress French, and think they are English."

The rich and famous of Buenos Aires are given the royal treatment even after death. Spaces at Recoleta Cemetery in Buenos Aires cost $20,000 per square meter. That's just 11 square feet!

TIMELINE

1536 - Pedro de Mendoza arrives in what is now Buenos Aires.

1580 - Juan de Garay tries to settle the area.

1776 - Buenos Aires is made the viceroyalty of the Río de la Plata.

1806 and 1807 - British troops invade Buenos Aires.

1810 - Buenos Aires declares independence.

1880 - Buenos Aires becomes the capital of Argentina.

1916 - Hipólito Irigoyen becomes the first president elected by popular vote.

1976 - A military junta seizes power.

2001 - Poor economic conditions cause riots in Buenos Aires.

BUILDING A CITY

European colonization of Buenos Aires dates back to 1536. That year, Spanish explorer Pedro de Mendoza arrived with 16 ships carrying almost 1,600 men. After conflicts with the native Indians, they abandoned the area.

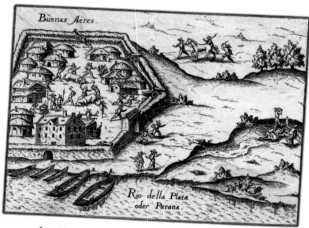

An illustration of Buenos Aires as an early settlement shows the hard life of the colonists.

Spanish explorer Juan de Garay led settlers to the area in 1580. But, the Spaniards did not allow Buenos Aires to become a major port. So, those who lived there resorted to smuggling and trading with towns farther inland. They traded herds of cattle and horses that grazed on the fertile Pampas.

Buenos Aires slowly grew. Soon, Spain recognized the city's valuable location. In 1776, it made Buenos Aires the capital of the region. Spain called it the **viceroyalty** of the Río de la Plata. But, Buenos Aires remained under Spanish rule.

This four-sided pillar called an obelisk was built in the Plaza de la Republica to honor the founding of Buenos Aires.

British troops invaded the area in 1806 and 1807. The *porteños* fought them off. In 1810, residents of Buenos Aires declared their independence from Spain. In 1816, the surrounding areas also professed their freedom. They formed an unstable group of **provinces**.

The provinces often fought among themselves for control of the entire group. So, Buenos Aires struggled to create its own independent government. A strong leader soon asserted his power. In 1829, Juan Manuel de Rosas became **dictator** and seized power. He remained in power until 1852.

By the late 1850s, Buenos Aires became the center of government in the area. Bartolomé Mitre was president when Buenos Aires became Argentina's capital in 1880.

In 1916, Hipólito Irigoyen became the first president elected by popular vote. But troubled times were on the way. A worldwide **depression** hit in 1929. Then, the military overthrew Irigoyen. This started a series of **coups**.

In 1946, Juan Perón emerged as a stable leader. Perón and his wife Eva worked hard to improve the lives of Argentines. However, they both had many enemies as well as supporters.

Rosas was supported by the Mazorca, a secret police force that murdered his opponents. Rosas fled the country when Justo José de Urquiza led a rebellion against him.

11

Perón won a second term in 1951, but he was kicked out by the military. He was elected again in 1973, but died the next year.

In 1976, a military **junta** seized power. Armed forces and police hunted down all who resisted. This was called the Dirty War.

During the Dirty War, most who resisted were tortured and killed. Between 10,000 and 30,000 people vanished without a trace. Many of the military leaders involved were brought to justice under the next president, Raúl Alfonsín.

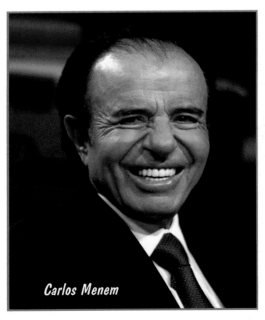

Carlos Menem

By this time, the **economy** in Buenos Aires was in very poor shape. Each new president has worked to fix the situation. In 1989, Carlos Menem took office five months early to start the work. However, Fernando de la Rúa still inherited the economic problems when he became president in 1999.

Economic troubles remain for Buenos Aires. This makes running the country very difficult. Argentina had four presidents in 11 days during 2001! Today, residents of Buenos Aires wish for stability. Many hope Nestor Kichner, the president elected in 2003, will be a good change for the country.

Nestor Kichner

EVITA

One of the most powerful political figures in Argentine history rose to fame after her husband became president. Eva Duarte was a radio actress. She was married to Juan Perón, who was elected president in 1946.

Evita, as she was nicknamed, created a social welfare foundation. This aided charities, hospitals, homes for the elderly, and schools. Evita also fought for women's right to vote. Families and the working class, whom she called "shirtless ones," worshipped her.

Evita never had an official government post. She made an unsuccessful attempt to serve as vice president of Argentina in 1951. She died in 1952, and her fame has only grown since her passing.

POWERS THAT BE

The town hall in Buenos Aires

The people elect the president of Argentina. The president governs the entire country with the help of a legislature. The federal government represents all 23 **provinces**, plus Buenos Aires. As the capital of the country, Buenos Aires is its own district.

The president of Argentina used to appoint the mayor. But today, the mayor is elected by the people. A mayor governs Buenos Aires with the help of a council. Sixty elected members make up the council. They work in the city, as do all members of the federal government.

Many famous government buildings and attractions are located in Buenos Aires. One of these is the Casa Rosada, or Pink House. This is a large, pink presidential palace built between 1862 and 1885. As a symbolic center of the city, the Casa Rosada is a favorite spot for tourists and residents.

The president of Argentina no longer lives in the Casa Rosada.

SCARY ROADS!

Some of the first sites tourists see in Buenos Aires are the many buses zipping around town. This is a popular way for residents to get to and from work, or just to get around on weekends. The buses drive fast, though, so passengers need to hold on tight.

Getting around by car in Buenos Aires is also popular. But, it can be a little risky. Cars in Buenos Aires go as fast as the buses. This is one reason why biking on the city streets is not very safe!

But, residents can take a safer route on the subway. The subway in Buenos Aires opened in 1913. It is a quick, easy way for *porteños* to go about their day.

For more leisurely transportation, many residents of Buenos Aires walk. A stroll through the grand avenues or many parks is a favorite way for *porteños* to travel at their own pace.

Opposite Page: *Buenos Aires's wide roads with many lanes of heavy traffic can be scary for tourists.*

MONEY TROUBLES

Demonstrators near the Casa Rosada protest economic conditions.

As the hub of the agricultural industry, the Pampas help ensure that Buenos Aires is Argentina's top trading center. Exports include beef, hides, wool, and wheat. In the city, factories produce clothing, leather goods, foods, and food oils.

Buenos Aires also has a large service industry. Many *porteños* work at insurance companies, banks, and stores. New shops on Calle Florida, a street just for people on foot, sell books, clothing, leather goods, and **souvenirs**. Tourists from around the world shop here.

Even with the city's strong trade, money continues to be scarce. Argentina's **economy** has declined as unemployment increased. In 2001, people rioted in the streets of Buenos Aires to protest conditions.

GAUCHOS

The Pampas cover an area larger than Texas. Like that state's cowboys, gauchos once rode on horseback, keeping watch over cattle on the plains.

Gauchos spent exhausting days alone on the open range. They lived on beef roasted in pits and yerba maté, an herbal tea. But, the days of the roaming gaucho are over. The countryside is divided. Gauchos have no choice but to work for those who own the land. Today, these South American cowboys star as folk heroes in novels, poems, and songs.

Gauchos patrol the Pampas.

HUMID CITY

Buenos Aires stretches along the western bank of the Río de la Plata. River breezes give the city a **temperate** climate. Year round, the weather in Buenos Aires is **humid**. In fact, about 35 inches (89 cm) of rain fall throughout the year.

Summer in Buenos Aires lasts from December to February. This season is hot and humid. Winter lasts from June to August and is also humid. But the weather is mild. Snow fell only once in the 1900s! So, Buenos Aires is a favorite winter vacation spot for people from colder climates.

Many porteños visit beaches to beat the heat.

During spring and fall in Buenos Aires, the weather can change rapidly. Rainfall in the city is heaviest during the month of March. This causes a lot of problems for *porteños*. Rainwater often floods low-lying neighborhoods.

PORTEÑOS

The population of Buenos Aires reached 1 million by 1900. Today, that figure has expanded to about 12 million! *Porteños* such as the mestizos share a blend of **unique** origins. Mestizos are people of European and American Indian background.

A blend of languages can also be found in Buenos Aires. Spanish is the official language of Argentina. Many residents of Buenos Aires also speak English, Italian, German, and French. A local dialect called *lunfardo* mixes Italian and Spanish words.

A Buenos Aires student

Some *porteños* learn a second language in school. Primary and secondary education in Buenos Aires is free, and all children must attend. After this, many students go to universities.

La Boca is the neighborhood that many people picture when they think of Buenos Aires.

The University of Buenos Aires is Argentina's oldest school. It was founded in 1821. It is also the largest university in Latin America. Almost 220,000 students attend. They have a choice of 1,000 courses offered each year.

BARRIOS

Buenos Aires is divided into 48 barrios, or neighborhoods. Each has its own flavor and history. La Boca is a fashionable, upscale port on the banks of the Riachuelo. Vibrantly colored houses contain artists' studios. The artists display their engravings, murals, and sculptures along Caminito Street. This pedestrian street resembles an outdoor museum!

San Telmo was also a fashionable neighborhood before yellow fever struck in the 1870s. At that time, many residents left the neighborhood. But today, several of its houses are restored, attracting artists and antique dealers.

When they aren't at school, children in Buenos Aires spend time with their families. Traditional families have a father as the head of the household and a mother to take care of the house. Today, many women have a career outside the home. In the city, most families live in apartments.

An important part of any family gathering in Buenos Aires is food. *Asados*, or "barbecues," are common at family parties and festivals. Beef is roasted over fires in open pits. Argentina is famed for its beef. Cattle are raised on huge ranches spread across the Pampas.

Beef roasting at a cattle market

Argentina is also famous for the tango. This dance combines long steps and graceful poses. It was first popular in working-class nightclubs. Today, people glide across the floor to tango music in dance halls, parks, and plazas. There's even a special festival on December 11 called Day of the Tango.

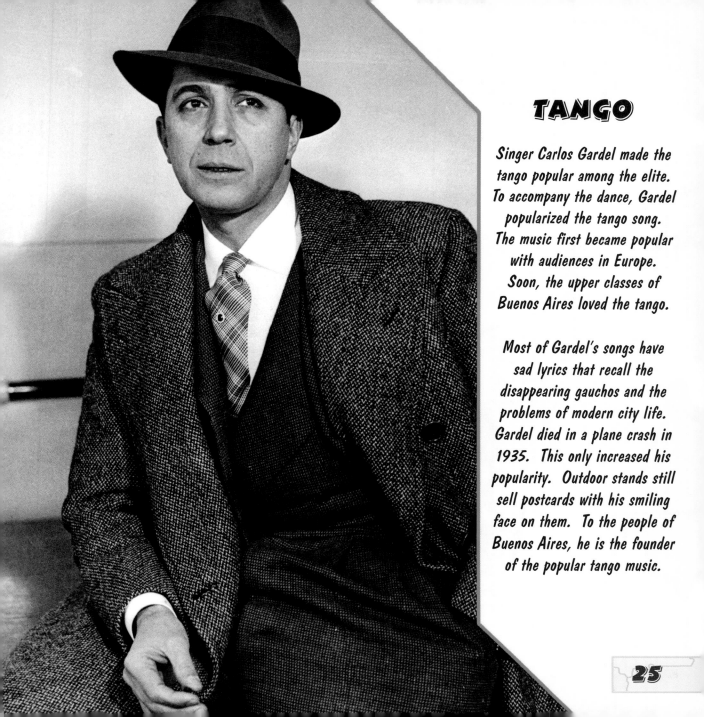

TANGO

Singer Carlos Gardel made the tango popular among the elite. To accompany the dance, Gardel popularized the tango song. The music first became popular with audiences in Europe. Soon, the upper classes of Buenos Aires loved the tango.

Most of Gardel's songs have sad lyrics that recall the disappearing gauchos and the problems of modern city life. Gardel died in a plane crash in 1935. This only increased his popularity. Outdoor stands still sell postcards with his smiling face on them. To the people of Buenos Aires, he is the founder of the popular tango music.

FREE TIME

At carnival time, the city celebrates with street parades. The carnival festivities in Buenos Aires are not as big as in some cities, but they are getting bigger. The celebrations and parades include dancers and drummers.

Buenos Aires residents also love to spend time playing and watching sports. Argentines are very good at playing sports with horses. They have been galloping through **polo** games at the Argentine Open Championship since 1893. Horse racing also attracts fans to the city.

The sport *pato*, or "duck," is similar to basketball on horseback. When gauchos played the game, they used a duck in a leather bag as a ball. Today, Argentines use a leather ball with handles. Two teams on horseback hurl the ball through baskets to score goals.

The Argentine soccer team celebrates after winning a match at home.

Soccer ranks as the top sport in Buenos Aires. British **immigrants** introduced soccer in the 1800s. Fans pack soccer stadiums every weekend. In Buenos Aires, eight teams battle for goals. Argentina won the World Cup in 1978 and 1986.

Many Buenos Aires residents enjoy gathering among the palm trees and gardens at the Plaza de Mayo. This huge square is the historic heart of the city. The Metropolitan Cathedral is also on the plaza. It was built in 1745. It contains the tomb of General José de San Martín, the "Father of the Nation."

Tourists also visit the tombs at the Recoleta Cemetery. Many of Argentina's rich and famous people rest there in more than 6,400 plots. The most popular site is Eva Perón's tomb. Splendid sculptures include pyramids and temples.

Another attraction for residents and tourists is the zoo. President Domingo Sarmiento founded the Jardin Zoologico in 1874. Native monkeys and birds are on display there. The zoo's mission is saving the Andean

Recoleta Cemetery

The polar bears are a popular attraction at the Jardin Zoologico.

condor. This huge vulture is the largest flying bird in the world. Its wingspan can extend up to ten feet (3 m)!

Other spots for seeing plants and animals include the botanical gardens and the zoo near Palermo. At Jardin Botanico, 8,000 plants from around the world grow. Like Buenos Aires, it is a good place to see the countries of the world represented in one small area!

GLOSSARY

architecture - the art of planning and designing buildings. A person who designs architecture is called an architect.

coup - a sudden, violent overthrow of a government by a small group.

depression - a period of economic trouble when there is little buying or selling and many people are out of work.

dictator - a ruler with complete control who usually governs in a cruel or unfair way.

economy - the way a nation uses its money, goods, and natural resources.

humid - having moisture or dampness in the air.

immigrate - to enter another country to live. A person who immigrates is called an immigrant.

junta - a committee that rules a country after the government is overthrown.

polo - a game played by two teams on horseback. Players use long-handled, wooden hammers to hit a small, wooden ball through their opponent's goal.

province - a geographical or governmental division of a country.

souvenir - an item that reminds a person of a certain place.

temperate - having neither very hot nor very cold weather.

unique - being the only one of its kind.

viceroyalty - an area that is ruled by a representative of a king or sovereign.

SAYING IT

Buenos Aires - BWAY-nuhs AR-eez
Fernando de la Rúa - fehr-NAHN-doh thay lah ROO-ah
gaucho - GOW-choh
Hipólito Irigoyen - ee-POH-lee-toh ee-ree-GOH-yayn
Juan de Garay - KWAHN thay gah-RAH-ee
Juan Manuel de Rosas - KWAHN mahn-WEHL thay RAW-sahs
Juan Perón - KWAHN pay-RAWN
Pedro de Mendoza - PAY-throh thay mayn-DOH-thah
porteño - pohr-TEH-nyoh
Río de la Plata - REE-oh thay lah PLAH-tah

WEB SITES

To learn more about Buenos Aires, visit ABDO Publishing Company on the World Wide Web at **www.abdopub.com**. Web sites about Buenos Aires are featured on our Book Links page. These links are routinely monitored and updated to provide the most current information available.

INDEX

A

Alfonsín, Raúl 12
American Indians 8,
    22
attractions 4, 15, 16,
    18, 19, 24, 26, 28, 29

C

climate 20, 21

D

Dirty War 12

E

economy 8, 10, 12, 13,
    18, 19
education 22, 23, 24
Europe 4, 8, 9, 10, 22,
    27

F

festivals 24, 26
food 18, 24

G

Garay, Juan de 8
gauchos 4, 26
government 9, 10, 12,
    13, 14, 15

H

housing 4, 24

I

Irigoyen, Hipólito 10

K

Kichner, Nestor 13

L

language 22

M

Mendoza, Pedro de 8
Menem, Carlos 12
Mitre, Bartolomé 10

P

Pampas 4, 8, 18, 24
Perón, Eva 10, 28
Perón, Juan 10, 12
Plata, Río de la 9, 20

R

Rosas, Juan Manuel de
    10
Rúa, Fernando de la
    12

S

San Martín, José de 28
Sarmiento, Domingo
    28
sports 26, 27

T

tango 4, 24
transportation 16